LOLA'S TRICK OR TREAT

DIANE deGROAT

HarperFestival®

A Division of HarperCollinsPublishers

"I'm going to be a Martian for Halloween."

"Just like you, Gilbert!"

"Me, too!"

"Don't be a copycat, Lola!"

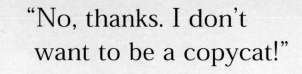
"No, thanks. I don't want to be a copycat!"

"Remember, Lola, you wanted to be a ballerina just like your friend Patti."

"I know!"

"I can't decide."

"I'll find a costume
in here. . . ."

"A firefighter?"

"A wizard?"

"A ghost?"

"I'll get it!"

DING DONG

"Trick or treat,
smell my feet!"

"Give us something good to eat!"

"What's wrong, Lola?"

"I want a costume no one else has!"

"Let's go trick-or-treating, Lola!"

"In a minute, Gilbert."

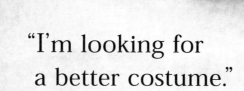

"I'm looking for
a better costume."

"Did you find
a costume, Lola?"

"Look, I'm a Gilbert!
Nobody else is a
Gilbert for Halloween!"

"Yes!"

"Happy Halloween, Lola!"